Everybody Hates
School Dances

everybody hates chris ™

Everybody Hates
School Dances

by Brian James

Simon Spotlight
New York   London   Toronto   Sydney

Based on the TV series *Everybody Hates Chris*™ as seen on The CW.

SIMON SPOTLIGHT
An imprint of Simon & Schuster Children's Publishing Division
1230 Avenue of the Americas, New York, New York 10020
™ and © 2007 CBS Studios Inc. All Rights Reserved.
All rights reserved, including the right of reproduction in whole or in part in any form.
SIMON SPOTLIGHT and colophon are registered trademarks of Simon & Schuster, Inc.
Manufactured in the United States of America
First Edition 10 9 8 7 6 5 4 3 2 1
ISBN-13: 978-1-4169-3562-9
ISBN-10: 1-4169-3562-2
Library of Congress Catalog Card Number 2006937728

Chapter 1

I stood at my locker, staring up at the poster hanging above it. I'd already read it so many times that I had it memorized. I knew everything I needed to know about the Spring Dance, which was just four days away, without having to read it off a poster. So why was I staring at it for the hundredth time? I guess I figured if I stared long enough, eventually some girl might walk by and ask me if I was going. Then I could make my move and ask her to go with me.

It didn't matter to me who my date was, just as long as she was a girl.

There was no way I was going to another school dance alone. And I wasn't going with a friend, either! I decided that at the Valentine's Day Dance in February—the second I got there, there was this photographer snapping pictures of couples under a giant heart made of flowers as they walked in. I got my picture snapped with my best friend, Greg Williger! I thought I'd never live that one down.

"So, Chris, who are you going to ask to the dance?"

I thought for a second that my plan had worked. Someone had asked me the question I'd been waiting to hear. But when I turned around, there wasn't a girl anywhere near me. It was only Greg. I tried not to look too bummed, but it wasn't easy.

"I don't know yet," I told him. "I was thinking I might ask Jen from our math class."

Greg's eyes lit up.

"How are you going to do it?" he wanted to know. He always got more excited planning these kinds of things than actually doing them. I think that's one of the reasons he had such a hard time actually getting a date. "Are you going to ask her in a note? Or maybe ask one of her friends? You need a plan."

I threw my hands up in the air. I had no idea. I wasn't even sure if I was really going to ask Jen, she was just the first girl who popped into my head. "I haven't thought about that yet," I told him.

"Well, when you do, let me know," he said. Greg wanted to ask this girl Vicki, who he'd had a crush on for almost two weeks, only he didn't know how to ask her. Greg thought if I came up with something good, then he'd use my idea to ask Vicki out.

"What about writing her a note, or asking one of her friends?" I said.

"Do you really think that would work?" he asked.

"How should I know? They were your ideas,"

I answered, rolling my eyes at him. I mean, he is my best friend and all, but sometimes Greg can be exhausting. Even so, I had to admit that both of his plans were a hundred times better than anything I'd come up with. They sure beat staring up at a poster, hoping someone would stop by and ask you why you were staring at it.

But as it turned out, those weren't even Greg's best plans. Those were just the spare plans that he was willing to lend to me. I listened to his other ideas as I opened my locker and took out the books I needed for my next class. He'd come up with a whole list of ways of asking Vicki to the dance. Most of them sounded more complicated than a lot of movies I'd seen. One of them even involved finding some way to save her life.

"Do you think I should wear a cape when I do it?" he asked me.

"That depends," I said. "Do you want to get beat up or do you want to ask Vicki to the dance?"

That's usually how I make all my decisions. Anything that can get me beat up is definitely not something I want to do. Wearing a cape is something that will get guys like me and Greg beat up for sure.

"Speaking of getting beat up," Greg said, and then he pointed over my shoulder. I turned around and saw Joey Caruso coming toward us.

Joey is the school bully of Corleone Jr. High. When he walks down the hall, everyone gets out of his way. I would get out of his way too, but usually he's coming for me.

I grabbed the last book out of my locker and closed the door as quickly as I could. Greg and I tried to get away before Joey reached us, but as soon as we took one step, him and his two friends had us blocked. There was nothing we could do except stay and listen to whatever he wanted to make fun of us for today.

I don't know exactly why Joey has it in for me.

I mean, he doesn't really like anyone, but he sure hates me. It doesn't matter what I do, he always finds some reason to pick on me. Anything I say, he turns it around to make it sound like I'm trying to start something. And if I keep my mouth shut, he says I'm trying to act like I'm better than him. So the only defense I have is to avoid Joey at all costs. But that day I was cornered, and there was no escape.

"Nice sweater, loser. Did you borrow that from your sister?" Joey said, pointing at me. I looked down at my sweater. Actually, it's a hand-me-up from my younger brother, Drew. I'm probably the only kid at Corleone Jr. High whose younger brother is bigger than him, but I'm not about to share that information with Joey. When I looked up, him and his friends were laughing.

"Yeah, ha-ha, very funny," I said, pretending to laugh. "Like I haven't heard that one before."

"Really? Then you must be deaf, because everyone can tell that's a girl's sweater," he said. That's what I mean by him twisting around everything I say. Trying to trade insults with Joey is like trying to play basketball against the Knicks. I stink at both. I'll always lose the game playing against pros like that. "But I guess that's okay since you run like a girl, and fight like a girl."

I always wonder why there are never any teachers in the hallway when I'm getting picked on. There always seems to be a teacher nearby when I'm doing something I'm not supposed to do. If I'm running through the hall, I make it three steps before one of them grabs my arm and tells me to walk. If I'm chewing gum, there's a teacher with a trash basket in front of my face telling me to spit it out before I even get to taste what flavor it is. But whenever Joey is getting ready to beat me up, all of a sudden all the teachers just disappear.

"Man, why don't you just leave me alone," I said. I knew it would never work, but I was really sick of listening to him make fun of me every day. Since I started at this school, every day is the same old thing. Joey finds something about me to pick on.

"Because you're a dork and I'm not. It's my job to let kids like you know how uncool you are." Then he pointed out my shoes, my haircut, and even the way I held my books as proof. By this time, there was a small crowd of kids standing around waiting to see a fight. All of them nodded with each thing Joey pointed out.

I couldn't take it anymore!

I was sick of being called a dork. So without thinking, I blurted out, "If I'm so uncool, how come I'm going to the dance in a limo, with the prettiest girl in Brooklyn?"

Everyone in the hallway stopped!

If I had yelled out, "FREE FRENCH FRIES!" I don't think I would've had more people staring at me than I did at that moment. That's because getting a limo for the school dance was just about the coolest thing anyone could do. And as soon as I realized that, I knew what a huge mess I'd just gotten myself into.

It didn't take long for everyone to gather around us. It felt like the whole entire school was now standing around my locker waiting to hear more about the limo that I'd just made up. There was no way I'd ever get a limo to take me anywhere, let alone to the dance that was just four days away. Even Greg was staring at me, wondering why I'd kept it a secret from him.

But Joey wasn't impressed. In fact, the one person I was trying to fool was the only person who didn't seem fooled at all.

"I don't believe you," he said. And I should've let it go right there. I should've played it off like a joke, even if it meant getting punched in the arm once before the bell rang. But there was just something about the way everyone was looking at me that made me want to lie some more. Because for the first time in my life, all the kids in the hallway were looking at me like I was just a little bit cooler than Joey.

"Then I guess you'll feel pretty stupid when I show up Friday in a limo with my date," I said.

"Who is she? I bet you don't even have a date."

He got me there.

I had to think of something quick.

"Uh . . . you don't know her," I said, buying some time to think. "She lives in my neighborhood" was all that I could come up with. But it worked, since I live way out in Bed-Stuy and none of the kids at school would ever be caught dead in that part of Brooklyn.

Luckily, the bell rang before I could make up any new lies to get me in more trouble. As all the other kids drifted to their classrooms, I leaned back against my locker. I had no idea how I'd ever get out of this alive. I looked up at the poster one more time and sighed. I now had four days to not only find a girl willing to go to the dance with me, but somehow find a limo, too!

"I thought you said you didn't have a date, or a plan? Where'd you find a limo?" Greg asked after everyone had gone.

"I made it up." Even Greg had believed my lie, but I'm not sure that was saying much.

"I don't know how you're going to pull this off," Greg said as we started heading to our next class.

"Yeah, me neither."

Chapter 2

Where I live, rumors spread faster than a fake flu outbreak on the day of a big test. All it takes is for one big mouth to find something out, and the whole neighborhood knows about it in a flash. Sometimes, it seems like people know all about the stupid things you do before you even do them! So the two hours I spent that day riding the bus to and from school were more than enough time for my lie about the limo to reach my block. The bus is slow to begin with, but put it in a race against a rumor and it's like an old lady in a wheelchair racing against a cop!

I should've known that word was out the minute I turned the corner. Everyone on my block was staring at me the same way the kids in school had been looking at me earlier. Well, almost the same. Only instead of seeing me as cool, the people on my block saw me more as dollar signs. I could see the old ladies leaning out of their windows wondering what I'd done to get rich. They probably thought I broke the law or something, but they were still wondering if there was any way they could get some of my newly discovered wealth for themselves.

"Hey, little man from across the street, come here a second!" someone shouted from behind me. That someone was Jerome, one of the older kids on my block, who is always trying to borrow money. When Jerome borrows money, he never plans on paying it back. Asking to borrow something is just a nice way of asking if he can steal it.

I took a deep breath and turned around. Jerome waved me over to where him and his friends were sitting on the stoop.

"Little man, let me borrow a dollar," he said.

I dropped my hands down at my sides. A dollar? Who'd he think I was, Daddy Warbucks? "I don't have any money." I sighed and waited for him to stop blocking my way so that I could go home and try to think of some way to fix the mess I was in.

"Sure you do," Jerome said. Then he looked at his friends and smiled before looking back at me. "We heard you got a limo picking you up Friday. So how about letting me borrow some of that limo money?"

I couldn't believe my ears! He didn't even know what day of the week it was most of the time, but he knew about a little lie I told only a few hours ago, all the way on the other side of Brooklyn? I mean, I knew that rumors spread fast, but before that moment, I never guessed they'd spread *that* fast.

If Jerome knew, that meant *everyone* knew. I was just hoping everyone didn't include my mom, because if she thought I was even considering wasting money on a limo, she'd make it so I wouldn't be going to any dances for the rest of my life. I had to get home before anyone had the chance to tell her!

"All I got is a quarter," I said, digging deep into my pockets. Jerome said that would do, so I handed it over. That was one less video game I was going to be playing. But I had other problems to worry about. Especially now that the neighborhood kids knew, I had to figure out some way to get out of this mess. It's one thing for the kids at school to think I'm a liar, but it's a whole different thing for the neighborhood kids to think that. In my neighborhood, being a liar is just about the worst thing you can be. Liars fall somewhere below thugs and just above drug dealers as the most hated people on the block, and I don't want that.

As I headed to my house, I tried to figure out

how to solve my problem. I had a grand total of ten bucks saved up. And even though I had no clue how much it cost to rent a limo, I knew it was a lot more than ten bucks. I tried to think of how I might be able to earn some money in the next four days, but the only things that would earn me that much money involved going to jail. No dance was worth that! Plus, even if I did earn the money, I still didn't have anyone to go with. This was shaping up to be the worst school dance ever.

And it was about to get a lot worse! When I got to my house, my little sister, Tonya, was waiting for me, and she knew all about it. Tonya is always looking for any way to get me in trouble. She thinks that as long as I'm in trouble, she can get away with anything. And she's right, too. She does get away with everything, because I'm the one always getting blamed.

She walked right up to me as soon as she saw me. Then she started poking her finger at me the way she always does when she's angry with me about something. "How'd you get a limo?" she demanded, poking me in the stomach. "Did you steal the money for it? I'm going to tell Mom and you're going to be in big trouble!"

"Will you be quiet? I didn't steal anything!" I said, pushing her hand off me and trying to pretend like I didn't know what she was talking about.

"If you didn't steal anything, then how'd you get it?" she asked, putting her hands on her hips and blocking me from getting inside.

"Mind your own business," I said.

"This is my business," she said. "Because if you get to take a limo to the dance, then the limo should take me to my birthday party that night, too! That's only fair."

My little brother, Drew, had been listening to us the whole time from the window. I guess he knew about the limo too, but it wasn't until he heard Tonya say she was going to get a ride in it that he became at all interested. "Hey, if she gets a ride to her party, then I'm getting dropped off at my friend's house in style to watch the Knicks game," he said.

At this point, I was getting real nervous that my mother was going to hear all of this. I wanted this to stay a secret for as long as possible. "Will you both keep it down?" I whispered at them.

"I'm not keeping nothing down until you promise me a ride to my party," Tonya snapped at me. So finally I had to tell them both that there was no limo and that I made up the whole thing. From Tonya's reaction, I couldn't tell which made her happier, thinking she was getting a ride to her friend's party, or knowing that I'd lied and having something to tell on me about.

"Ooohh, Mom's going to be so mad at you for telling lies. You know what she thinks about liars! She says liars are worse than thugs. Boy, are you going to get it!" And I had to grab her arm before she went in the house. Lucky for me, Tonya had one weak spot that could keep her from tattling. Candy!

To Tonya, candy is better than gold. Good thing it's cheaper, too, otherwise I'd have been in a lot more trouble than I could've handled. I told her I'd buy her a dollar's worth of candy if she promised not to tell.

"Make it two dollars and you got a deal," she said.

"Two dollars, are you crazy?" I didn't have two dollars to waste on her.

"MOM!" she shouted.

I covered her mouth with my hand as quickly as I could. "Fine, two dollars," I told her. That meant I was down to eight dollars for the limo.

"If she's getting candy, I want candy too," Drew said. "That's only fair."

"Fine," I said, "but I swear, neither of you better breathe a word of this to Mom!"

I went up to my room and got four bucks from my secret stash. I gave each of them two. I counted the six dollars that were left as they raced off to the corner store. I'd just bought myself a little more time to figure this whole thing out. But I was beginning to think all the time in the world wouldn't help. This was one disaster that I couldn't see any way out of.

Chapter 3

The next day at school, all the girls were acting a little more interested in me. It seemed that once they found out I had a date, they started looking at me differently. I guess they thought that if some other girl was interested in me, then maybe I was worth a second look. They whispered and smiled as I passed them in the hall, and I actually smiled back. It didn't matter to me that it was all based on a lie. At least not right then. I figured I might as well enjoy it while it lasted, because as soon as they all found out the truth, I'd go right back to being invisible.

As I headed toward the lunchroom, this girl Amanda stopped me. She touched me on the arm. No girl had ever touched me on the arm unless it was to push me out of the way. "Hi, Chris," she said, and gave me a little wave with her other hand. Then she gave me a smile that made my heart skip a beat!

"Hey, Amanda," I said. I looked over at Greg and his eyes were popping out of his head. Amanda is one of the most popular girls in our grade and she was talking to me! To us, it was nothing short of a miracle.

"So, who's this lucky girl you're taking to the dance?" she asked.

The girl I was taking to the dance? For a second I completely forgot about that. Then I came crashing down to Earth and remembered why she was interested in me in the first place.

"Oh, that girl," I said. "She's just someone I know."

Greg nodded and winked at me to let me know I'd done a good job covering.

"She's not your girlfriend, is she?" Amanda asked. Then she made her eyes look all sad and said, "I sure hope not."

I couldn't believe it! One of the prettiest girls in the school was jealous over me! If I'd had wings, I'd have flown right up to heaven. I could've died happy right then and there. The doctors would've taken one look at my face and told my mom not to worry, because her son had died the happiest boy on the planet.

"Um, no. She's not my girlfriend, just some girl I know," I told her, trying to play it cool. After all, a man had to keep his options open. I wasn't about to let myself get tied down to some girl who didn't even exist.

"I hope she doesn't mind if you save a dance for me," Amanda said.

"Yeah," I said. "I mean, no. She won't mind. Or she might, but that's okay." I was so confused that I didn't know what I was saying. Usually girls look at me like I'm crazy when I start speaking nonsense like that, but that time it only made Amanda smile more. She made me promise to save her a dance before she headed off in the other direction with her friends giggling alongside her.

I was so stunned that I wasn't sure if it had actually happened, or if I'd been daydreaming. But if I was daydreaming, then Greg was having the same dream. "I can't believe you just flirted with Amanda Hubbs!" he said.

"I did?" I asked, still a little confused. Then it hit me. "Yeah, I did, didn't I?"

"Dude, you're so in there," Greg said.

"I am?" I asked. I wasn't so sure myself, and besides, Greg says that to me at least once a week, and so far, he's never been right. But this time I thought he might be onto something.

"Of course you are. Did you see the way she was looking at you?" I had to admit that the way she was looking at me was pretty nice. "You can tell everything a girl is thinking from her eyes. And her eyes said she was jealous!"

I was on cloud nine as we walked into the lunchroom. Not even the horrible smell of cafeteria food was able to spoil my mood. That was until Greg reminded me that Amanda was jealous of a date I didn't have.

By the time we sat down at a table, all the joy I'd felt seconds before was gone. My stomach sank lower than it would have if I'd actually eaten the food they were serving. But then I had an idea. "What if I just ask Amanda to the dance? I could tell her I'd rather go with her, and that I canceled my fake date." That way I'd solve one of my problems, and then I could just focus on the other half of the wreck I was in.

"Are you crazy? You'll lose all your leverage! You have to concentrate on getting a date for the dance; that's the only way to keep Amanda from forgetting about you," Greg said. Then he explained that the only reason she was interested in me was because she thought I was taken. If I suddenly looked too eager, she'd stop caring about me.

"If you know so much about girls, how come you can't ever get one?" I asked, suddenly not so sure I should be taking Greg's advice.

"That's not true," he said. "I asked Vicki to the dance this morning and she said yes."

"Really? Why didn't you tell me?" I asked.

"I just did," he said.

"But how'd you do it?" I asked. We'd spent an hour talking about it yesterday; you'd think he'd be able to give me some details. Then I remembered his superhero idea and wondered if he'd actually gone through with it. "You didn't wear a cape, did you?"

"Nah, you were right about that. I definitely would've gotten beat up, and nothing impresses a girl less than getting beat up in front of her," he said.

I know all about that. I'm the king of getting beat up, and that also makes me the king of bad impressions with girls. But I had a chance to change all that if I could only get a date and then have the whole school see me dancing with Amanda. "So what *did* you do?" I asked Greg, thinking maybe it could work for me.

"I wrote her a note."

Writing a note was the one way I knew for sure wouldn't work in my neighborhood. If you start slipping notes into people's mail slots or under their doors, next thing you know you'll be dodging all sorts of things being thrown at you. The only things that ever get slipped under people's doors where I live are eviction notices or subpoenas. Either way, people will always chase you away with flying dishes first and ask questions later.

It was clear to me, though, that I didn't have time to come up with any complicated plans. I had to get a date fast. So I decided I would just have to come out with it and ask every girl I knew on the block. One of them was bound to say yes, even if it was just out of pity for me looking so pathetic. I could live with that if it meant I'd get to dance once with Amanda.

"Even if you get a date, there's still the limo problem," Greg pointed out.

"Don't remind me," I said.

I looked into it that night, and found out it cost about one hundred dollars to rent a limo. I only had six. But in my neighborhood, if you need something for cheaper than what it costs in the real world, you can always try to get it from Risky. Risky has ways around everything. I figured if it cost one hundred dollars in the real world, Risky could get it for twenty. There's always a catch, though. Usually the stuff he sells has something wrong with it. Any limo from him would probably need to be pushed.

But that was okay with me, just as long as the kids at school saw me getting out of it at the dance.

"Do you think I could borrow some money?" I asked Greg. Greg gets more allowance each week than I get in a month. If anyone has money to lend me, it's Greg.

"Man, I would, but I need all the money I got. Now that Vicki is going to the dance with me, I want to get her some flowers," he said. "Plus, I need to pick up some cologne so that I don't smell funky on our date."

"Thanks anyway," I said.

I'd just have to ask the girls in the neighborhood and not tell them about the limo. Then I'd tell everyone at the dance that the limo broke down. Now with the whole Amanda thing, getting the date was the more important part.

Chapter 4

That afternoon I went through my closet to pick out my best outfit. I must have tried on everything in there. At first I thought maybe a suit and tie would be best. Girls always seem to fall for a man in a suit! I pictured myself as the black James Bond, playing it super smooth as I walked up to the door. I wouldn't even have to say a thing. They'd open the door, see me, and beg to go to the dance with me. They'd fall all over me like in the Bond movies.

everybody hates school dances

But then I remembered the last time I wore a suit and tie, to my cousin's third wedding. I got my tie caught in the bathroom door and had to wait there until someone came to set me free. I imagined getting stuck in the door of the first house I went to. Every girl on the block would hear about it, and I'd never get a date.

The suit and tie were definitely out!

I flipped through some more clothes and came across my blue Adidas tracksuit. It was almost brand-new, another hand-me-up from Drew. I tried it on and looked in the mirror. Boy, did I look good!

All I needed were some finishing touches. So I combed out my hair and smoothed out the edges. Then I splashed a little bit of my dad's aftershave on my face and I was ready to go. I tried on a pair of sunglasses, too, but when I looked in the mirror again I was afraid I looked too good. People would think I was there to rob their house if I showed up with my eyes hidden behind a pair of dark shades.

So I took those off, took a deep breath, and tried to work up the courage to actually go through with my plan.

As I got ready to leave my bedroom, I really hoped there were still some girls on the block who hadn't heard about the limo. I wasn't going to mention it. I didn't see any way I was ever going to get one. I'd just make sure we showed up to the dance an hour early and then tell everyone at school that they must have missed it. It might not fool Joey, but it was worth a try.

But then my mind went blank when my mother started shouting my name.

"CHRIS! CHRIS!" she hollered.

She yelled so loud, I could feel my bedroom door shake. When she's angry, her yelling can register as an earthquake. I'm always surprised the fire department and the police rescue squads don't rush over to our house to see if it's still standing.

"CHRIS, GET DOWN HERE!" she yelled again.

She was always ruining everything. I tried to think of what I'd done this time. Maybe I'd forgotten a chore, or didn't pick up milk, or maybe it was any of a thousand things Tonya had made up, but whatever it was, I had to try to get it out of the way as soon as possible. The clock was ticking and I was down to three days. I couldn't afford to waste another minute.

"Coming," I mumbled, and headed out of my room.

I practiced my walk down the hallway. To be cool you have to have a good walk—something with a little stutter step in it is always the best. A really cool walk could make everybody freeze in their tracks as I passed by. But it was me who did the freezing once I saw my mom standing at the front door.

Outside our door was a line of girls, with their mothers, all dressed in their best Sunday clothes. I wondered what was going on. Was my mom having some sort of party that I didn't know about? But when they saw me, they all started waving and calling my name, asking me to pick them as my date. I thought I must have hit the lottery or something until I heard them start arguing with one another. Each girl was telling the others that they weren't classy enough to be seen in a limousine. That's when it hit me! Those girls wanted nothing to do with me. They just wanted a ride in my limo, and all their mothers just wanted their girls to be dating somebody rich. It just happened that they all thought I was that somebody.

My mouth dropped open and my eyes popped out of my head!

And then there was my mother's face! She glared at me so hard, I thought flames were going to shoot out of her eyes right then and there.

"Boy, what are all these people banging on my door for, thinking you got some limo taking you to a dance on Friday?" she said, stomping her foot as she asked.

I gulped, trying to think of something to say.

"I might have let it slip out at school," I said.

"Oh, you might have let it slip, huh? I might let my hand slip across your head and smack the stupid out of you," she said. She's always threatening to smack the stupid out of me. I don't know why she never does. I sort of wish she would—then maybe I'd stop getting myself into so many bad situations.

Then she turned to the crowd gathered outside. She sent them all away, telling them I wasn't going to be seeing anyone this afternoon, and possibly not any other afternoon ever again. I could see Tonya laughing at me from the living room. "Told you you was going to get in trouble," she said as she ate a piece of candy that my money had paid for. I gave her a mean look, but she just stuck her tongue out and showed me the candy she was eating to remind me that my bribe money had been wasted since Mom had found out anyway.

When she finally got everybody to go home, my mom shut the door and came straight to me. "What's the matter with you, telling lies like that? You know that's how criminals start out! You start by telling those kinds of lies and next thing you know we're visiting you in jail," she said. "Is that what you want? You want to go to jail?"

My mom thinks every bad thing I do is somehow going to land me in jail. By her logic, every kid I know will be behind bars by the time he turns sixteen. I know better than to say that to her, though. I know better than to say anything at all.

I kept my mouth shut. I was too bummed to explain the whole thing about Joey, and how everyone just happened to overhear and how the bell rang before I could tell the truth. It didn't matter, though. I was doomed. My mom hadn't told all the girls and their mothers that I'd lied because she was afraid of what they'd think of me. But by not telling them it was a lie, they still thought I had a limo coming on Friday, which meant there was no way I was ever getting any of those girls to go to the dance without one.

No limo, no date.

And both of those added up to me getting a good whipping by Joey Caruso and having him embarrass me in front of the whole school. Amanda was certainly never going to talk to me again either. I guess I was going to have to get used to being a nobody again for the rest of the school year.

Chapter 5

At dinner my mom hadn't cooled off one bit. Her face was hotter than the meat loaf steaming in the pan. When my mom gets this way, my dad always keeps real quiet until he's sure that she isn't mad at him. He never comes right out and asks because if she's mad about something he's done and he doesn't know what it is, he'll end up in worse shape than he started out in.

Once she'd finished filling everyone's plate, my

mom turned to my dad. "Did you hear what your son Chris did today?" she asked. Whenever I get in trouble, I'm always *his* son. On the other hand, if I do something good, I'm 100 percent her kid.

My dad smiled and looked relieved. "Oh, *Chris* did something?" he asked, happy to find out he was off the hook. Then he quickly stopped smiling and made his face look serious again. He looked over at me and I looked down at my plate. "Well, what did he do?" he asked.

"I'll tell you what he did," my mom said. "Your son told everyone that he had a limousine picking him up here at our house for his school dance just so he could impress the girls! Can you imagine that? A limo? At thirteen years old? I've never even ridden in a limo!"

That wasn't exactly the truth. I only told one person, but everybody else sort of found out. And plus, I didn't say it to impress a girl. I said it to keep from getting beat up. The way I see things, any lie is okay if it keeps you from getting your butt kicked.

My dad started to smile again. I couldn't believe it! He wasn't even mad. In fact, he had to stuff his mouth full of food to keep from laughing.

"Is there something funny about all of this?" my mom asked.

"Not really," my dad said.

"Then *why* are you laughing?"

Then my dad smiled some more and he started to laugh a little. Drew started laughing too, not because he knew what was funny about the situation but because my dad's laughter was contagious. I even cracked a smirk, but I didn't dare laugh. Unlike them, I sat within striking distance of my mom's hand. Along with threatening to smack the stupid out of me, my mom also threatens to smack the smile off my face at times like these. If she caught me laughing, she'd have smacked my smile clear across the room. I would have watched it fly right out the front window and land on the street. People wouldn't even have been freaked out seeing it there. They'd say, "Looks like that Chris boy got his smile smacked off again."

After a minute, my dad was able to stop laughing. By that time, my mom had pushed her chair away from the table and folded her arms in front of her stomach. She wanted an explanation, and for my dad's sake, I hoped he made it a good one.

"Oh, come on, Rochelle," he pleaded. "Don't be like that."

"And why shouldn't I be like this? Your son does something terrible and all you do is laugh about it," she said. I have to admit, I was a little relieved that for the first time since that afternoon she was angry at somebody else.

"I just don't see what's so terrible about it," my dad said.

"Oh, you don't? Maybe you will once we're spending all your days off visiting your son in jail because you taught him that there wasn't anything wrong with lying." I thought for sure my dad would cave after that. But he didn't. He told my mom that this was different.

"I used to tell girls all sorts of things to impress them," he said. "Once I even told a girl I was a fighter pilot, and I hadn't ever been in an airplane before."

I couldn't believe it. My dad was actually taking my side. Tonya couldn't believe it either. She looked as upset as my mom. My dad even told me he might be able to help out! He said he had a friend who owed him a favor. "He's got this car he'd probably let me borrow," my dad said to me.

"A real limo?" I asked in disbelief. My plan was actually starting to come together!

"It's not *exactly* a limo," my dad said.

Oh no! My stomach sank. I knew that *not exactly* really meant *nothing at all* like a limo. But I was fresh out of options. It was either take my father's help and hope for the best, or pretend to be sick the night of the dance.

"You got a date?" my dad asked me.

"Not *exactly*," I admitted. My dad told me I'd better get one real quick, because he was going to have that car waiting out front for me on Friday evening. My mom just shook her head, and my dad did his best not to make eye contact with her.

"Thanks, Dad," I said. I knew how much trouble he was going to go through to help me out, and I didn't want to seem disappointed. Besides, I never said what kind of limo I was taking to the dance, so no one could say that I lied if I showed up in something that was almost like a limo. I didn't say it couldn't be a converted limo, did I?

Next thing I knew, the table erupted with noise. Tonya and Drew dropped their forks and started shouting at the same time.

"If Chris gets a limo to take him to the dance, then I get to take it to my birthday party!" Tonya shouted.

"Yeah, and I should get a ride to my friend's house to watch the game," Drew added.

My dad held up his hands and told everyone to quiet down. He said there'd be plenty of room for all of us. "Even for us," he said to my mom, telling her that after dropping all of us off, the two of them could go out to dinner, and she'd finally get a ride in a limo.

That sure made her happy, and got my dad out of the doghouse. I can't say it was so great for me, though. Because even if now I was showing up in a limo to the dance, I was also showing up with my whole entire family inside! And limo or no limo, showing up to a school dance with your whole family in the backseat was just about as uncool as it gets!

Chapter 6

The next morning, I headed out of the house feeling pretty confident that I would be able to get a date. My dad had called his friend the night before. He was going to pick up the limo after work the next day. Everything was starting to come together. It looked like I was going to get away with the biggest lie I ever told.

I still needed to ask a girl before I got on the bus to head for school, though. I wasn't too worried about that. I just needed to find one of the girls who'd stood outside my door the day before and ask her. In fact, there was this girl who I'd liked for a while and I was sure I saw her standing out there. Her name is Ariel and she lives right near the bus stop. So I headed over to her house, hoping it wasn't too early to knock on her door.

Lucky for me, she was already sitting on her front stoop, braiding her little sister's hair. When I saw her face, all my nerve left me. Even with the limo, she was still too pretty to want a date with me. She was so pretty that just thinking about her saying yes made me forget all about Amanda or any other girl.

I stood on the sidewalk staring at her. I couldn't make my mouth work. I tried to tell my brain to start talking, but nothing came out.

"Ariel, why is that boy staring at us?" I heard her little sister ask.

Ariel looked at me. If she'd been standing outside my house the day before, she sure didn't seem interested anymore! "Yeah, why *are* you staring at us?" she asked me.

"Um . . . I . . . ah," I stumbled, forgetting why I was even there in the first place.

Ariel grabbed her sister's hand. "Come on, let's go inside," she said.

I saw my big chance fading fast. So I worked up the courage and held up my hand. "Wait," I said. Ariel stopped and looked at me over her shoulder. She raised her eyebrows and waited for me to speak again. "My school's having a dance tomorrow. Do you want to go with me?" I asked.

She bit her bottom lip and gave me a good long look. It felt like the whole world stopped as I waited for her to answer.

"I'm not sure," she said. "Can you dance?"

Could I dance? She wanted to know if I could dance? Wasn't the limo enough?

But looking at her, standing there in the morning

sun, I wanted her to go to that dance with me so bad it hurt. So I nodded my head up and down, even though I'm the worst dancer this side of the East River!

"Are you sure you can dance? You don't look like much of a dancer with those skinny legs of yours," she said.

I looked down at my legs. I didn't know how she could tell what kind of a dancer I was just by looking at my legs. They didn't look too skinny to me. But I had to think of something, so I said the first thing that popped into my head.

"Um . . . that's because I'm a break-dancer," I said. It was sort of true. The last time I tried to dance, I almost broke my arm. "In fact, I'm the best break-dancer in all of Brooklyn!"

I might have gone a little overboard with the last part, but I didn't want to take any chances.

"You can break-dance? That's so cool," Ariel said. Her eyes lit up like sunshine. I was so blinded by them that I didn't even think about what kind of trouble I'd be in once she found out I couldn't dance at all. But I decided to deal with that when the time came. It's always better to deal with one problem at a time. Besides, I'd seen enough break dancing in the subway that I was pretty sure I'd be able to fake it.

"Okay, I'll go to the dance with you, Chris," she said. I nearly fainted. She told me to pick her up at seven o'clock sharp. "I want all my friends to see me get into that limo! I can't wait to see their faces."

"Seven o'clock," I repeated. "I'll be here."

She waved good-bye as she went into her house. I was so happy that I ran all the way to the bus stop. Nothing was going to bring me down. I couldn't believe how it was all working out. First my dad came through with the limo, and then the prettiest girl in Brooklyn agreed to go with me. I made something up, and then it came true. Maybe I needed to start making up things all the time. I could tell people I was a millionaire, and maybe three days later I'd really be one!

As I waited for the bus to come, I decided to practice a few dance moves. I remembered one move I saw this guy do in Prospect Park. He folded his arms in front of him, dropped to his knees, lay down, and then spun around on his back. It looked easy enough. So I tried it.

I folded my arms.

I dropped to my knees.

And then I fell right on my butt!

Two old ladies who were waiting for the bus let out a yell. They thought I'd dropped dead. Then they rushed to my side and hovered over me. "Boy, you okay?" they asked. They were checking my pulse and holding their hands in front of my mouth to make sure I was breathing.

I finally told them I was fine. "I was just dancing," I mumbled.

"Dancin'?" they shouted in amazement. Then they both rolled their eyes, looked at each other, and started laughing. "That's no kind of dancin' I ever saw," the one said. "Boy, you better give up on dancin' altogether before you hurt yourself."

Too late for that!

I rubbed the pain out of my back. It was probably better not to try that move again. I looked back to my street to make sure no one there saw me. If Ariel had caught me falling down like that, she would have canceled our date faster than it took me to hit the ground. But there wasn't anyone watching except those two old ladies. The coast was clear. I'd just have to come up with some easier moves before tomorrow night.

Chapter 7

I was at my locker when I saw Greg coming down the hall. As soon as he got near me, the air turned funky. "What's that smell?" I asked, holding my nose.

"It's my new cologne," Greg said. "It's pretty sweet, huh? The guy at the store said it'll drive the girls wild."

"More like drive them away," I said. "That stuff's nasty."

Greg took a sniff of his shirt. Then he made a face. "That's what I thought at first, but it's growing on me."

Stink was what was growing on him, but I didn't have the heart to bring him down. Besides, there were more important things to discuss than his body odor. I still had to tell him all about how things fell into place.

He couldn't believe it when I told him. "You're so lucky," he said. "You got nothing to worry about. After tomorrow, you're going to be, like, the coolest kid in school."

"As long as nobody sees me break-dance," I said.

"Why would they? You can't break-dance," Greg said. "I've seen you dance. You're terrible! I'm a better dancer than you, and I'm white."

"I know that," I said. "But Ariel doesn't. She thinks I'm the best break-dancer in Brooklyn."

Greg pointed at me and asked, "You, a

break-dancer? Why would she ever think that?"

"Because I sort of told her I was," I admitted, feeling a little bit guilty about it now that I had time to think about what I'd said.

Greg shook his head. "You really don't know when to stop, do you?" And there was nothing I could say, because he was right. Maybe my mom was right. This lying thing was contagious, and it just kept getting me into trouble. So I promised myself I'd start telling the truth from that moment on. I had to stop telling lies or I might really turn into a criminal. There was no way I wanted to end up in jail!

When I saw Amanda walking toward me, I decided to start with her. "Hey, Amanda," I called. She stopped and smiled. When she came over to me, she touched my arm just like she did the day before. It made me forget why I'd called her over in the first place.

"You still saving me a dance?" she asked.

It came back to me as soon as she mentioned dancing. "That's just it," I told her. "About that, I was thinking it wouldn't really be fair to my date."

"That's too bad, Chris. I was really looking forward to dancing with you."

As she started to walk away from me, I wondered if she'd ever touch my arm like that again. "Maybe next time," I called out, but she just kept on walking. I knew then and there that there would never be a next time.

I don't think Amanda had ever been turned down before in her life. That's because I was the only one stupid enough to do it! She had let go of my arm right away. Truth was, I felt pretty bad about it, but I knew I was doing the right thing.

"Are you crazy?" Greg shouted as he punched me in the arm. "You just rejected the most popular girl in school!"

"I know what I'm doing," I said. But I didn't really.

everybody hates chris

I thought I did, but as Amanda was walking away, I couldn't help feeling like I'd made a mistake. But I promised myself no more lies, and I was going to try to stick to it. Anyway, Ariel was much prettier and I really liked her. I wasn't about to mess that up too.

"Well, it might work out for the best anyway," Greg said. Then he explained how once word got around that I turned down Amanda, all the girls would be after me. "Playing hard to get always works," he said.

"I don't really care, as long as Ariel doesn't run off when she sees me dance," I said.

"How hard could it be?" Greg asked. Then he told me to just fake it. I told him how I tried that at the bus stop before school. I was still sore where I'd landed.

All I had to do was learn two or three moves, and I'd be home free. I'd go to the park after school and watch the dancers there. There had to be some things I could learn in one night. And if I did, for the first time in my life I'd avoid being embarrassed at a school dance!

As we headed to class, Greg reminded me that I could always do the robot dance. All I had to do was stand there and look like I had no rhythm. And he was right—that was something I could do without even trying.

Chapter 8

By Friday afternoon I still hadn't learned a single dance move. I practiced in my room as much as I could, but it was no use. Soon it would be time to get ready for the dance. It was hopeless.

"What are you doing?"

I turned around to see Drew standing in the doorway. He had his eyebrows raised and a look on his face like he'd just smelled something rotten. I guess he caught a whiff of my dancing.

"None of your business," I hollered.

"I hope you weren't trying to dance," he said. "Remember last time? You nearly broke your arm."

"Why don't you just get out of here?" I didn't want him to watch me. It was bad enough that I had to see myself in the mirror. I didn't need anyone else to see.

"All I'm saying is, if you dance like that, everyone's going to laugh at you," he said as he walked out of the room. There was nothing I could say. He was right. I had no moves whatsoever. I'd just have to stall the whole night. Maybe I'd get lucky and they wouldn't play any music that was good for break dancing. And if they did, I'd just have to tell Ariel I needed to go to the bathroom, and pray they didn't play another one.

I didn't have time to fool around anymore. I had to get ready. My dad had already left to pick up the car from his friend. He was going to stop by our house first and pick up Tonya, Drew, and my mom. Then he was going to pick me up at Ariel's house at seven o'clock.

"Chris, you better hurry up and get dressed," my mom hollered from the hallway.

"I know!" I shouted. For the dance, I was going to wear a suit. I decided to just leave the tie at home—that way nothing could go wrong. My mom had ironed the pants and shirt for me earlier, so all I had to do was put them on. Then I combed out my hair, smoothed it down, and took a last look in the mirror.

I looked good. Real good.

I glanced at the aftershave. Then I thought about how Greg had stunk earlier that day, so I left it right where it was.

My mom was waiting in the living room with the camera. She started snapping pictures as soon as I walked in the room. "Look how good my baby boy looks," she said. Then she started fussing with my collar and straightening out my jacket. "Go stand with your sister. I want to get a picture of you two."

I made a face. So did Tonya.

"Come on, Mom, do you have to?" I asked.

My mom stomped her foot. "Yes, I have to. It's not every day my babies are all dressed up," she said.

"Fine," I mumbled. "But could you *please* not take any pictures with Ariel? It's embarrassing."

"Stop complaining and get over there by your sister," my mom said. I didn't argue. I'd better let her take all the pictures she could then, or else she'd just take them later when it would be worse.

I stood next to Tonya. She was all dressed up for her party and she was smiling as wide as she could. My mom aimed the camera and snapped a picture. I put on a fake smile and she snapped some more. After that, she had Drew take one of me with her. Then another. Then she had him take some more with Tonya in the picture with us. Next she had Tonya take some with me, her, and Drew. Before I knew it, I was blind from the flash going off in my eyes so many times!

I was still wiping my eyes when I walked out the front door. My mom said they'd be over in a few minutes. I kept my fingers crossed, hoping that when they did show up, they stayed in the car.

Chapter 9

There was a whole crowd of people standing outside Ariel's house when I showed up. All her friends were lined up waiting to see her get into a limo. When they saw me approaching, they all turned toward me. I'd never had so many people staring at me before without having done something stupid first. I wasn't used to it. I thought maybe my zipper was down or something. But when I checked, it wasn't.

That's when I realized that I'd become the star of the block. Even Jerome and his friends were impressed. "Hey, little man. Looking good," he said. He held up his hand to give me a high five. I felt like the starting center for the Knicks! I thought to myself that this must be what it felt like to be famous. I thought it wouldn't take me long to get used to that feeling.

I made my way through the crowd, giving out high fives and getting slaps on the back. I heard the girls whispering and their mothers grumbling about how I hadn't chosen any of their daughters. I was full of confidence. Nothing could bring me down!

I strutted up the stairs to Ariel's front door and rang the bell. Her mother answered the door. She was grinning from ear to ear. Then she pinched my cheek and told me how cute I looked. I asked her if Ariel was ready, and she told me it would just be a second.

It felt like an eternity! That was how I learned that when a girl says she needs a second, what she really means is that she needs at least ten minutes!

But as soon as I saw Ariel, I knew that the time I spent waiting and being pinched and stared at was all worth it, because she was gorgeous. She looked even prettier than the first time I saw her, last summer, in her bathing suit running through the fire hydrant. At the time, I didn't think that was possible. But it was, because she looked a million times better than that as she walked out the front door.

"Hi, Chris," she said.

Man, my heart melted on the spot. I was in love!

"You look . . . uh . . . nice," I said. Then I bit my tongue. I couldn't believe out of all the words to choose from, I chose *nice*. Old ladies were nice. Candy was nice. *Nice* certainly wasn't the word to describe Ariel, and she knew it too.

"Nice? You think I look nice?" she asked, putting

her hand on her hip and squinting her eyes at me. One thing I'd learned from watching my dad deal with my mom was that I'd better come up with something quick. Compliments to girls were like answers on a test—there was always a right one and a wrong one. Ariel's look let me know I'd come up with the wrong one!

"I meant, pretty. Really pretty," I said quickly.

"That's more like it," she said, and started smiling again. It was a close call, but I'd passed the test. Things weren't starting off on a good note, however.

But if I thought that part went bad, I was in for a huge surprise after what happened next!

Just as we made it down the steps, there was a loud sound from down the street. It sounded like fireworks going off on the Fourth of July. Everyone turned to see what it was except me. I already knew. With my luck, it could only be one thing. Our limo!

I turned my head and there it was—a big old school bus that had been painted white and had the windows tinted black. On the front of it was a Rolls-Royce medallion that looked like it had been ripped off a real Rolls-Royce and superglued on. And every time my dad switched gears, it backfired so loudly I was afraid it was going to blow out the windows.

Ariel turned and gave me the meanest look I ever saw. "That ain't no limo," she said.

I tried to play it cool. "It's sort of like a limo," I said. "It's big and has lots of seats and lots of windows."

She wasn't buying it.

"I'm not getting in that thing!" she said. Then she pulled away from me and stormed back up the steps. Her mother was standing there shaking her head. This same lady who had been pinching my cheeks moments before was telling her daughter how she always knew I was no good. She put her arm around Ariel and led her inside. The slamming of the door was almost as loud as the backfire from the bus!

I was left standing out there all alone. I heard the crowd start whispering again. Only this time it wasn't the good kind of whispering. It was the kind of whispering I usually heard at school when I'd tripped in the hallway or something like that. But still, it was nothing compared to the whispering that was going to happen when I showed up to the dance in that bus without a date.

I was ruined!

That's when Drew stuck his head out the window. "Hey, Chris, this thing is so cool. You gotta come inside," he shouted. Then he looked around. "Where's your date?" he asked.

Before I could say anything, this girl Felicia in the crowd stepped up next to me. "Is that your brother, Drew, in there?" she asked. "I didn't know he was going." I was about to explain that he was getting dropped off at a friend's house, but she grabbed my arm before I could. "I'll go with you," she said.

I knew she was only saying that because she liked Drew. All the girls on the block like Drew. Felicia isn't pretty like Ariel. And she's nowhere near the prettiest girl in Brooklyn. She isn't exactly ugly, but she's close. Even I'm a good catch for somebody like her, but at that time I was in no position to argue. She was my last chance. So I kept my mouth shut and climbed aboard with my new date. At least I didn't have to worry about break dancing anymore. It almost made the embarrassment of being stood up worth it.

Chapter 10

It wasn't long after we got on the bus that Drew told Dad that his friend's house was coming up. We were going to drop him off before going to the dance since his friend was so close to our house. When Felicia heard that, the smile disappeared from her face. I tried to look away, but she got right in my face.

"What does he mean, drop him off?" she asked me. "He ain't coming with us?"

My mom waved her hand in front of her face and laughed. "Oh no, child, you don't have to worry about him bugging you two all night," she said. Of course my mom had no idea that having Drew around to bug us all night was the reason Felicia agreed to go in the first place.

I felt bad, but it wasn't totally my fault. She never gave me the chance to explain. So I just shrugged my shoulders, unsure of what to say. Felicia rolled her eyes at me and shook her head. I'm used to that, though—it seems like every girl has that kind of reaction to me.

But she got over it pretty quickly after we dropped Drew off. By the time we got close to the school, she seemed to have forgotten all about him, and I thought maybe my luck was changing for the better again. Felicia even scooted closer to me on the seat. "I guess I could have a good time with you anyway," she said. At that moment, as we bounced through the streets of Brooklyn in a tacky school bus, it was just about the nicest compliment I could get.

My dad made the final turn and I could see my school. I was really going to pull it off. I might not become the coolest kid in school afterward, but at least nobody would be able to say I lied. Sure, maybe I exaggerated a lot, but they couldn't say I lied and that was enough for me.

"Besides, I can't wait to see you dance," Felicia said. "Ariel bragged about it all day yesterday."

My jaw fell to the floor! I knew this was too good to be true. Now not only was my limo a bus, but I had ruined my chances with Amanda for a girl who blew me off. And on top of worrying about Joey beating me up for the whole limo thing, Felicia wants to see me break-dance?

Tonya spun around in her seat. I saw that look in her eye and knew what she was about to do. She burst out laughing just as we pulled up in front of the school. I quickly stood up and covered her mouth before she could say anything about my dancing. I took Felicia's hand and led her to the door. Before he pulled the handle to open the door, my dad reminded me that he'd be back there at ten o'clock to pick us up. "Okay, Dad," I said, and the door flung open.

It felt like every kid at my school was standing out front just waiting for me to show up. And when they saw that cartoon-looking bus roll up, they broke out in fits of laughter!

"I've never seen a limo like that before," one of the kids said.

"That's what they call a *ghetto*-sine," another kid teased.

I tried to ignore them as I made my way in, but it was impossible to ignore the *bang* that went off as my dad started up the engine again. The whole crowd ducked as if a bomb had gone off. Once they realized what it was, the laughter was louder than before. And to top it all off, my mom poked her head out the window and snapped one last picture. Tonya poked her head out too and started chanting,

"Chris and Felicia sitting in a tree . . . !" I wouldn't have thought it possible, but the laughing got even louder after that.

I wanted nothing more than to find a dark corner and hide for the rest of the night. But even that was too much to ask for. As soon as we entered the gym, we bumped into Amanda. She took one look at Felicia and made a face. "You wouldn't dance with me because of her?" she said.

Felicia got right up in her face. I covered my eyes. I didn't want to see this.

"That's right! You got a problem with that?" she yelled, rolling up her sleeves like she was getting ready for a fight. Out of all the girls on my block, I had to end up with the one girl who can fight better than me.

There wasn't going to be a fight, though, because Amanda couldn't have cared less about me anymore. "I don't have a problem," she said. Then she turned to her friend and whispered, "Did you see that *thing* that he called a limo?" and they all started giggling.

Felicia wasn't about to let them make fun of me. Where I come from, making fun of someone's date is the same as making fun of them. And it didn't matter to Felicia that she didn't want to be there with me to begin with; it only mattered that she was there and she had her pride to protect.

"You can make fun of his limo all you want, but you won't be able to say nothing after he shows all of you up on the dance floor," she said.

"Chris can dance?" one of Amanda's friends asked. They were wondering why none of them had ever seen me dance before.

"Are you kidding? He's the best break-dancer in all of Brooklyn!" Felicia said. And just like when I'd blurted out about the limo four days earlier, everyone fell silent and all eyes were on me.

Felicia made everyone move out of the way, ignoring me when I asked her to stop. I looked at

Greg. I made a face to let him know I needed his help. I was in a big jam and I couldn't think of anything. Greg understood and came to my rescue.

"Uh . . . he can't just yet," Greg said. "He needs to wait for the right song."

I nodded. "Yeah, I need the right song," I said. Then I gave Greg a wink to let him know he really saved me this time.

It was working. The crowd was starting to drift away. Then I noticed Joey. He looked really mad that I'd actually pulled it off. Seeing his face gave me some satisfaction. I was beginning to have a good time and he knew it. There was no way he was going to let me off the hook.

I saw him whisper to his buddies. Then I watched him make his way over to the stage where the DJ was. He leaned over and said something. Then the DJ stopped the music and I knew I was in trouble.

The DJ got on the microphone. "We have a special request," he said. "I've just been told we have one of the best break-dancers in the city here tonight." I looked for the bathroom and got ready to run, but all the kids started cheering and pushing me to the center of the dance floor.

"I just love to watch break dancing," the DJ continued. "So as a special treat, we're going to have a half hour of nonstop breakin' beats!"

The spotlights came on and were pointed right at me. I just stood there as the music started. Greg whispered good luck as he backed away. There was nowhere to run. I knew I was about to become the biggest fool Corleone Jr. High had ever seen. . . . I could only hope that I didn't break any bones doing it!

If you liked
Everybody Hates School Dances,
check out an excerpt from book #2,
Everybody Hates Romeo and Juliet!

Chapter 1

It was a morning just like any other morning at my house. I woke up to hazy sunlight streaming through my bedroom window. I heard the soft hum of buses echo through the streets. The radiator clanked and hissed a soothing rhythm. All was peaceful. I lay in bed, stretching lazily, enjoying the calm. Then I closed my eyes again and dozed off. . . .

"CHRIS! CHRIS!"

Like I said, it was a morning like any other morning.

"CHRIS!"

My mom was shouting—right in my ear, her hands cupped close to my head to muffle the sound. She didn't want to wake my dad. But clearly she wanted *me* wide awake and ready for action.

"What?" I said.

"What do you mean, what? What are you doing still in bed?" Mom demanded. "You know it's Monday morning. It's seven forty-five. Your father's already home and sleeping."

I groaned. My dad must have unplugged my alarm clock when he came in. He likes to do that sometimes, to save on the electric bill.

Drew and Tonya, my younger brother and sister, poked their heads into the room.

"Mama, we're gonna be late for school," Tonya whined.

That girl loves to whine. If there was a Whining

Olympics, she'd win gold, silver, *and* bronze.

"Chris, get dressed!" my mom ordered. "Get something in your stomach too. Then hurry up and walk your brother and sister to school."

I rushed to get my clothes on and banged my toe on the dresser. "Ouch!" I yelled out.

"Hush up now!" Mom hissed. "You know your father's sleeping."

How could I forget? Mom makes sure we never forget that my dad works two jobs—and that he needs his sleep during the day.

Quickly and quietly, I got ready. Drew and Tonya watched. Mom tapped her foot impatiently. I hate an audience when I'm getting dressed. I rushed into the bathroom.

Yup, I thought. Typical Monday morning at the Rock apartment, in Bed-Stuy, Brooklyn, where early morning peace can't last past 7:46.

A little while later, I walked quickly down the street with Drew and Tonya. I'd moved so fast back in the apartment that we were right on time now. There was no real reason to hurry. And I was in no rush to get to school. But I was in a hurry to get rid of my brother and sister.

Every morning I have to take Drew and Tonya to school. They go to the one in our neighborhood. Lucky them.

I have to go to the junior high school clear across Brooklyn. Why? My parents are convinced I'll get the right sort of education there.

So right after I dropped off Drew and Tonya, I got on the number 26 bus. Then I transferred to the 44. By the time that bus stopped near Corleone Jr. High in Brooklyn Beach, I was the only black face around—on mass transit . . . in the streets . . . and without a doubt, in school.

I'm thirteen years old. I want to blend in with the crowd, not stand out like a Knicks fan at a Celtics game. All for a better education, my parents said. An education in getting my behind kicked, is a better way to put it.

At the school entrance, Joey Caruso brushed past me. Hard. "Watch where you're going," he growled.

No doubt about it. A typical Monday morning. What would it be like to start the week without the school bully getting on my case? I'll probably never know. Ducking my head, I kept going down the hall.

"Hey!" My friend Greg Williger opened the locker next to mine. Greg's white. Except for that, we're a lot alike—short and skinny. And used to getting picked on. "Did you catch the *Star Trek* marathon on TV last night?" he asked.

I sighed. "No." Greg just can't understand why everyone isn't a Trekkie. He can go on and on about that show, like it's the most important thing to happen to civilization since sliced bread.

"Well, it was great. The first episode was the one where Captain Kirk . . ."

Greg kept talking as we went into our homeroom and sat down. "And then the teleporter broke down and . . ."

I yawned.

"So Spock said . . ."

"Ahem." The teacher, Miss Cassio, cleared her throat. "Good morning, class. There are a few announcements I need to make, so I'd like quiet."

"And then the Romulans—"

"Quiet," Miss Cassio repeated.

Greg finally got the hint.

"Now," Miss Cassio said as she shuffled some papers, "a reminder from the custodian: Repeated flushing of toilets will cause them to overflow. Only one flush per student is allowed."

She flipped to another page. "Anyone found writing on school property will be suspended."

"But, Miss Cassio, what about the blackboard? That's school property," a girl in front of me said.

"This means graffiti, Lauren," Miss Cassio said,

in a way that made it clear she didn't want to be interrupted again.

Quickly she turned to another page: "The cafeteria will be closed this week, by order of the Health Department."

A few kids cheered at that one.

Finally Miss Cassio turned to the last page. "There will be auditions for the school play next week."

An excited hum went through the class. "Maybe it's a musical," Lauren said.

"I can't wait!" said another girl named Tammy. "Finally!"

I shook my head. School plays interested me as much as *Star Trek* did.

"Anyone interested in trying out can pick up a copy of the play." Miss Cassio pointed to a pile of papers on the corner of her desk. "And put your name on this list." She waved a sheet of paper in the air.

Tammy raised her hand. "What's the play?" she asked.

"*Romeo and Juliet.*"

Shakespeare? We were doing William Shakespeare? I knew a little about his plays. They were written about four hundred years ago. Some were funny, but lots were tragedies, filled with death and dying. The only black character I knew about was Othello—and he didn't make it out alive.

I sank down in my seat as all the girls in front of me sighed dreamily.

"I love that play," Lauren said. "It's so romantic. Star-crossed boyfriend and girlfriend, and all that. It's beautiful, but incredibly sad. Like, Romeo and Juliet have such a true love. And what happens?"

Danny, one of the popular boys in class, put his hands around his throat and made a choking sound.

Lauren glared at him, but in a kind of adoring way. She thought he was cute.

"All right, class," Miss Cassio said. She tapped

the sign-up sheet. "I'll post this by the door after homeroom. You don't have to decide now. But if you know you want to try out, come on up."

Almost all the girls rushed up to Miss Cassio's desk. The boys just sat there and looked at one another. Then Danny stood up. He stretched lazily, like he had all the time in the world. Then he walked to the front of the room. Then five or six boys followed him.

Surprise, surprise. Maybe this Shakespeare play was a cool thing to do after all. But the characters spoke in weird, complicated sentences, and instead of saying "you," they'd say "thee" or "thou." *And* all the guys wore tights! Uh-uh. Definitely not for me.

"What do you think?" Greg nudged me.

I shrugged and said, "I think I'm not going to do it."

The bell rang, and everyone shuffled out of class. I walked out, expecting Greg to be right behind me. He wasn't. He was signing the audition sheet.

He caught up to me in the hall. "This is going to be great." He grinned. "*Romeo and Juliet* has all the drama of a really good *Star Trek* episode."

He stopped and looked at me. "It would be even greater if you tried out too."

"Me?" I squeaked. No way was I going to be in a play where boys wear tights. The humiliation! The itchy legs! "No," I said, walking away.

"Come on," Greg said. "It will look good on your college applications."

"No."

"You can see your name in lights!"

"No, no, no."

Greg pulled on my arm to stop me. I brushed him off and started walking again.

"You'll make your mom proud!"

I just rolled my eyes at that one, not even bothering to answer.

"It's a sure way to get girls!"

I stopped. Was it really? Of course, movie stars

are always surrounded by women. But they also drive expensive cars and live in mansions.

Up ahead, a group of girls were talking excitedly. "I can't wait to try out," said Tammy.

"I would give anything to be Juliet," Lauren said dreamily.

"Me too, me too!" they all squealed.

"Who do you think will be Romeo?" Tammy asked.

Lauren pretended to swoon. "I don't know. But it has to be somebody cute! And hot!"

They surrounded Danny and the other boys who'd signed up, asking questions and joking around.

What if I were Romeo? Would they swarm around me, too? There was only one way to find out.

I turned to Greg. "I'll do it!"